Hazel

Robyn's Best Idea

Illustrations by Yvonne Cathcart

First Novels

The New Series

Formac Publishing Company Limited
Halifax, Nova Scotia

Formac Publishing Company Limited acknowledges the support
of the Cultural Affairs Section, Nova Scotia Department of
Tourism and Culture. We acknowledge the financial support of
the Government of Canada through the Book Publishing Industry
Development Program (BPIDP) for our publishing activities.

We acknowledge the support of the Canada Council for the Arts
for our publishing program.

National Library of Canada Cataloguing in Publication Data

Hutchins, H. J. (Hazel J.)
    Robyn's best idea

(First novels. The new series)
ISBN 0-88780-531-0 (bound) - ISBN 0-88780-530-2 (pbk.)

    I. Cathcart, Yvonne II. Title. III. Collection

PS8565.U826R619 2001	jC813'.54	C2001-900197-5
PZ7.H96162Rob 2001		

Formac Publishing
Company Limited
5502 Atlantic Street
Halifax, NS B3H 1G4

Distributed in the United States by:
Orca Book Publishers
P.O. Box 468 Custer, WA
U.S.A. 98240-0468

Distributed in the U.K. by
Roundabout Books (a division of
Roundhouse Publishing Ltd.)
31 Oakdale Glen, Harrogate,

Printed and bound in Canada

N. Yorkshire, HG1 2JY

Table of Contents

1
Who's There?

It was while we were eating supper that Mom first heard the scratching and scrabbling sound in my bedroom.

"What's that Robyn?" Mom asked.

"Nothing," I said. I popped a meatball into my mouth. Sweet and sour meatballs are my favourite.

Thump went the thing in my bedroom.

"Nothing again," I said. "Don't worry about it."

Mom was already getting up from the table. I finished

all the meatballs on my plate as quickly as I could.

"Robyn!" said Mom, opening my bedroom door. "There's a cat in your bedroom!"

"A cat?" I jumped up from the table and hurried to the door. "There *is* a cat in my bedroom! How did it get there!"

"Robyn..." said my mom.

I reached down. The cat was small and grey with a cream-coloured streak above one eye and a white bib under its neck.

"Someone must have let it in while we weren't home," I said. I petted it. It started to purr. "Maybe the landlord let it in. Or maybe the Kellys next door."

The cat rubbed against Mom's legs.

"And it likes you!" I said.

"Robyn," said my mom, "you know we're not allowed pets in the apartment."

"We babysat Aunt Meg's cat for a whole month," I said.

"That's when we found out about the no-pets rule," said Mom. "Remember?"

"This is a very quiet cat," I said. "The landlord will never know it's here."

Mom ran her fingers through her hair. Suddenly she looked very tired. "Robyn," she said. "We're on shaky terms with the landlord these days. I missed work because I was sick last month. We're a bit behind with the rent."

"We are?" I asked.

"We'll be able to catch up next month, but we have to stay on the landlord's good side," said my mom. "I'm sorry Robyn."

I could tell by the way she said it that she really was sorry. And I know how much she worries about bills and rent.

"No problem," I said.

I picked up the cat, slipped my jacket over both of us, and headed out the door.

2
No Cats for Us

OK — I knew how the cat got into my bedroom.

I even knew I wouldn't be able to keep it, at least not forever. But I thought I might be able to keep it for a couple of days.

It was just one of those crazy ideas I get sometimes. I especially get them when the teacher has "My Life" time at school.

My Life is when we bring something from home that we'd like to talk about. It happens the last week of every month. When it does, Jessica Johnson starts going overboard. She's about the richest kid in school and she brings in all sorts of amazing stuff.

I don't like having to bring something from home. It makes me feel queasy inside just thinking about it. I don't have neat stuff lying around the house that I can just pick up and bring. I don't have the latest toy, or a pet guinea pig, or a wood rose my grandma sent from Hawaii. I don't have a grandma that goes to Hawaii.

I have to think really hard to find things to bring to school. I have to think so hard it hurts my brain.

Last month I took the plant my mom and I started from seed. The month before that, I took my photographs from the summer. This month I was thinking of taking a small grey cat with a streak over one eye and a white bib. But how can you take something that isn't yours, even for a few days?

I carried the little cat out the back door of the building and into the alley.

"Hey, Robyn!"

Ari Grady was coming down the back alley. At school Ari is part of a gang my best friend Marie and I call the three twerps, but on his own he's OK.

"When did you get a cat?" asked Ari.

"I didn't," I said, setting the cat down. "We can't have cats in our apartment. I'm just letting it go."

"Here?" asked Ari.

"This is where it came from," I said.

"It must be a stray," said Ari. "Poor little cat. I could take it home except my whole family is allergic to cats." His eyes were watering even as he petted it.

"It'll be OK," I said. "It's been around here all fall. It doesn't seem to mind."

As if to prove my point the little cat leapt to a patch of sunlight on the fence and happily began to clean itself.

"It's a really cute cat but if I could have any pet in the world I'd want something else," I said. "Something like a snapping turtle."

"Or an alligator," said Ari.

"Or a Tyrannosaurus Rex!" We both laughed.

Then Ari went home.

I don't think Ari is allowed any pets either.

3
Water Snakes
and Bubble Gum

The next day was Monday.
Three kids brought things
from home. One of the kids
was Jessica Johnson. Can you
guess what she brought? An
iguana about as long as the
teacher's desk!

An iguana! Ari and I were
joking about having a
dinosaur for a pet and Jessica
really had one! Well, almost!

Except I wasn't joking. If I
could have any pet in the
world, I really would choose a
reptile. I know they aren't

cute and fuzzy but I'm really interested in the way they move, the feel of their skin and the way their eyelids work. Reptiles are amazing!

When I saw that iguana walk across our classroom like something from a million years ago I felt really strange inside. Jessica's not even interested in reptiles the way I am! How could she have one?

"And how can she fit something that big in her bedroom?" I asked my best friend Marie at recess.

"You haven't seen her bedroom," said Marie.

"Have you?" I asked.

"Yup," said Marie. "Her bedroom is huge. Her whole house is huge. The iguana

probably has its own bedroom."

"And neither of them have to worry about the rent," I said.

"What?" asked Marie.

"Never mind," I said.

On the way home from school I bought some bubble gum at the store. Bubble gum always makes me feel better. I was going to buy three pieces, but I'd forgotten about the tax so I had to put one back. Brother.

I wandered around the store chewing half a stick of bubble gum. With only two pieces, I had to make it last. Of course you can't blow much of a bubble with only half a stick.

That's when I saw the box

of plastic water snakes.
Plastic water snakes are great
to take to school. They go
scooting across the room and
everyone laughs. The teacher
can't get mad either because
there's a scientific principle
behind it — kind of. And no
one had brought a plastic
water snake this year.

I held the water snake in
my hand and gave it the
tiniest squeeze. Blip — it
jumped into the pocket of my
coat. Water snakes do that sort
of thing. Blip — it jumped out
again. Blip — in again. Blip
— out again. I decided to quit
while I was ahead. I put the
snake back on the shelf and
headed out of the store.

Near the door I ran smack

into Jessica Johnson. She was buying a large slush and about three pounds of bubble gums.

"Hi Robyn!" she said. "Want a bubble gum?"

"No thanks. I don't like them much," I said.

And I headed home.

4
One Big Mess

Some people have bags of money. Bags and bags and bags.

They don't have to worry about landlords and rent.

They don't have to worry if they've got enough to cover the sales tax on ten cents worth of bubble gum.

They don't have to worry about finding something interesting to bring to school.

That night I dreamed about having bags of money myself. A small grey cat with a streak over one eye and a white bib

knocked on my door and gave it to me. I was rich, rich, rich. The next day I brought an entire circus to school.

Actually that's not what I dreamed, but it's what I told my best friend Marie. It was the next day at school. I was hoping she'd say something like "Yeah, and that would sure show Jessica," but she didn't.

I had to say it instead.

"That would sure show Jessica," I said.

"Show her what?" asked Marie.

"You know — show her — for all the fancy stuff she brings when it's My Life time in class."

Marie shrugged.

"Jessica's OK if you give her a chance. And we don't have to bring anything fancy."

"What are you going to bring?" I asked.

"My brother and I made a robot last night," said Marie. "He's not electric — we used egg cartons and elastic bands and popsicle sticks — but he's kind of cute. The robot I mean. Not my brother."

Marie made a face. She doesn't like her brothers, but I guess sometimes she builds things with them anyway.

"That's what I'm bringing. Why don't you make something too?"

After school I got out all the popsicle sticks I've been saving at home for the last five years. I decided to make a castle. It would have towers, dungeons and a drawbridge. I worked on it for what felt like hours.

In the end I only made the drawbridge and one crooked wall that kept falling apart. I covered the entire kitchen table with glue.

A water snake was looking better all the time.

When my mom came home from work she took one look at the table and ran her fingers through her hair again.

"I'm sorry," I said. "I'll clean it up."

"I'll help you," said my mom. "You need to rethink this project, whatever it is. But take a break first. Maybe

Marie can play until supper."

Mom was right. I needed to rethink my project. But it didn't have anything to do with Marie.

5
Meow

"I'll be back in time for supper," I told my mom.

I headed downstairs and out into the back alley. My feet weren't taking me towards Marie's house. My feet were taking me towards the store — the store with the water snakes that jump into people's pockets almost by accident.

"*Meow.*"

Half way down the alley, the little cat came running to meet me.

"Go home," I told it.

"*Meow.*"

It rubbed against my legs.

"Go away," I told it.

It followed me around the corner and onto the sidewalk.

"*Meow. Meow. Meow.*"

Cats don't know a lot of different words.

"Go back," I told it.

"*Meow.*" It followed me.

Far at the end of the block I could see the store. It was on a busy street. Traffic was going every which way. How does a cat cross a busy street in the city anyway? I didn't want it to follow me. I didn't want it to get squished by a car!

I stopped. The cat stayed right beside me like it was guarding me. Maybe it thought it was Lassie the

Wonder Dog. How do I know how a cat's brain works? All I know is that some cats are very stubborn.

"All right," I said at last, "we'll go home."

"*Meow, meow, meow.*"

The little cat didn't sound any happier, but at least it was walking away from the busy street.

We sat on the back step of the apartment together. We sat there for a long time, long enough for me to think about what was really bugging me. It wasn't having to take something to school. It wasn't even Jessica Johnson.

What was really bugging me was the difference between Jessica and me. I

couldn't figure out how some
families have lots of money
and other families don't have
as much even though they are
smart and work hard and are
good people too.

"OK," I said to the cat. "Most of the time I'm good. Sometimes I think of stealing water snakes from the store. But I didn't actually do it."

"*Meow*," replied the cat.

I agreed. If we sat there for a thousand years I wasn't going to figure out the answer. I didn't think anyone else was going to figure it out real soon either.

I went back inside. I was glad I hadn't stolen anything, but I still didn't know what I was going to take when my turn rolled around on Friday.

6
Two Great Ideas

On Wednesday, Marie and Jessica both had their names on the blackboard for My Life presentations.

Marie brought her robot. It was a zillion times better than my castle.

Most robots don't have ears but this one did. When she moved the robot's arms, its ears wiggled. It looked a lot like Marie's brother, the one who helped her build it. Weird.

Jessica had already brought something on Monday so I

couldn't figure out why she brought something on Wednesday too. But she did. Guess what it was — a water snake.

A water snake! Just like I'd been looking at in the store but three times as big and with neon colours. I couldn't believe it! The snake slid and flipped around the class. The teacher went into a regular science lecture about it.

I told the Kelly twins all about it that evening.

"When you're old enough to go to school, don't ever get into a class with someone named Jessica Johnson." That's what I told them. "And stay right away from teachers that do something called My Life."

The Kelly twins live in the apartment next to us. They're eight months old. Most kids my age don't have friends that are eight months old, but I do. I've helped out with the Kelly twins since they were tiny babies.

These days the Kelly twins can crawl across the floor, play peek-a-boo and giggle like crazy. I was playing with them while Mrs. Kelly was having a bath.

We were playing hide-the-ball-under-the-cushion-and-be-surprised-to-find-it-there. Little kids play little games. That's OK. I'm used to the Kelly twins.

"You three are certainly having fun tonight," said Mrs.

Kelly when she came out of the bathroom.

The twins were smiling identical smiles and laughing identical laughs. It was like looking at one person in a mirror, except they were both very real. Sometimes I am amazed at how alike they are.

Suddenly I had a brain wave.

"Mrs. Kelly," I asked, "do you think the twins could come to school on Friday? It's my turn to bring something from home."

Mrs. Kelly looked surprised.

"I don't mean that I'd hold them up in front of the class like they were a rock collection or something," I said. "They could just be special guests for a little while."

Mrs. Kelly looked at the twins. They smiled happily back at her.

"I think they'd like that, Robyn," said Mrs. Kelly.

Hurrah!

7
Spots

All Thursday I planned the twins' visit.

I'd talk about Abigail holding my finger. I'd talk about being the first person to see them roll over.

I'd show the twins the mobiles hanging from the ceiling and the fish tank at the back of our room. I wanted Abigail and Angela to have fun too.

When I got home from school, however, the phone rang.

"I've got bad news,

Robyn," said Mrs. Kelly. "The twins have spots. It's chicken pox."

"Oh no," I said.

"We won't be able to come to school tomorrow," said Mrs. Kelly. "I'm sorry. It seemed important to you."

But that wasn't what I was worried about. When they were just babies the twins were so sick they had to go to the hospital.

"Will they be alright?" I asked.

"Chicken pox is very gentle on babies," said Mrs. Kelly. "It's you I'm worried about. Older kids can get a lot sicker. And a lot spottier."

As I hung up the phone, I was glad the twins would be

OK. I wasn't even upset about them not being able to come to class. But I couldn't help thinking just a little about tomorrow. People with chicken pox don't have to stand up in front of the class and give silly talks.

All evening I watched for spots. I looked at my arms. I looked at my stomach. No spots.

But the next morning they were there — chicken pox everywhere.

"Are you sure?" asked my mom.

"Don't come near me," I called from my sick bed. "You'll get it too!"

Mom looked puzzled.

"What's going on Robyn?"

she asked.

"Chicken pox!" I said. "Stay back!"

Mom left the room. She returned with the phone, the thermometer and a glass of apple juice.

"I'll leave these here, just in case," she said. "I'll trust you to do what's right. But Robyn, you've already had chicken pox. You don't get them twice. And there is the lid to a red marker under your bed."

She left me there! My own mother knew I was faking and she left me there!

This isn't the way mothers are supposed to act. What if she started to act like this all the time?

It was too mixed up for me. I washed off the red spots, dressed and headed down the apartment stairs.

I didn't have anything to bring to school. I didn't care. Well, I did care but it was too late now.

It wasn't until I opened the back door of the building that I realized the whole world had changed.

8
Hairy Pig?

Snow!

I'd been in such a rush I hadn't looked out the window to see what the day was like. A blanket of white had fallen overnight — the first snow of the year. It made everything clean and beautiful. The whole world smelled wonderful. I was suddenly glad I'd decided to go to school.

Then I saw the little cat. The snow didn't make everything wonderful for the little cat. It was sitting all fluffed up in a dry spot beneath an overhang. There were no paddy paw prints around it. It must have spent the night right there.

All night beneath the overhang! Ari was right. It was a stray. It didn't have a home. For the first time I began to think about what that meant.

"Are you all right?" I asked.

"*Meow*," it said. But it didn't come out.

I spent all first period thinking about the cat.

I spent all second period drawing in my math notebook.

When third period arrived, I hadn't got a lot of school work done. I was feeling a little bit nervous too. Three other kids gave their talks. Then it was my turn.

"Robyn?" asked the teacher.

"I haven't brought anything from home," I said, "but I've drawn a picture I'd like to talk about."

"That would be just fine Robyn," said the teacher. "This is your few minutes to use however you like. You don't really have to bring something from home."

Now she tells me.

But even if I'd known, and even though I was more nervous than I usually am when I talk in front of the class, I wouldn't have changed what I was going to do.

I made my way to the front of the room. I took a deep breath. This wasn't exactly the way My Life talks were supposed to be.

"There is a very nice stray cat in our back alley," I said. "Now that winter is here, it really needs a home."

I held up my picture — one small grey cat with a streak over one eye and a white bib.

"That doesn't look like a cat! That looks like a hairy pig!" said Grant, number one twerp.

"This isn't the lost and found department, you know!" said Linden, number two twerp.

But Ari, number three twerp, gave me the way-to-go

sign behind their backs.

Marie took the robot out of her desk and made its ears wiggle in support.

And Jessica Johnson called out, "Cut it out you guys. Robyn's trying to help."

I didn't know she would be on my side!

9
A Good Home

"Did you find something to take to school today, Robyn?"

Mom and I were eating supper.

"How did you know about that?" I asked.

"I saw Mrs. Kelly in the hallway," said Mom.

"How are the twins?" I asked.

"They're going to be just fine," said my Mom. "What about school?"

"I talked about the little cat that doesn't have a home," I said. "It's a nice cat. Maybe someone will adopt it."

I didn't sound as hopeful as I wanted to sound. The picture really had looked like a hairy pig. Who would want to adopt a hairy pig?

Just then the doorbell rang. Jessica Johnson was standing in the hallway.

"Hi, Robyn," she said. "Dad and I got your apartment number from the mail box downstairs. I hope that's OK."

Jessica's dad was coming down the hall. He was carrying a box. Why would Jessica bring a box to my place?

"*Meow*."

Inside the box was a small cat with a streak over its eye and a white bib.

"Is this the cat you talked about in class?" asked Jessica.

"This is it," I said. I scratched the top of its head. "But I'm trying to find someone to adopt it, not someone to return it to me. We aren't allowed pets."

"I'm wondering," said Jessica, "is it OK with you if I adopt it?"

Jessica Johnson wanted the little cat! She was asking me about it! My mind started moving a million miles a minute.

"Would you feed it the right food?" I asked.

"Yes," said Jessica.

"Would you take it to the vet?" I asked.

"Yes," said Jessica.

"Would you make sure your iguana doesn't eat it?" I asked.

"I gave my iguana to my cousin. I don't like iguanas," said Jessica. "But I love cats. I'd take really good care of it. I'd name it Meow, just like it says. Is it OK?"

I looked at Jessica. She has more money than I do and sometimes that makes me mad. But I think Marie is right. If you give Jessica a chance, she's OK. She really would take good care of the little cat. And Meow was the perfect name.

"It's great," I said.

"Thanks, Robyn," said Jessica. "Thanks a lot!"

"*Meow.*"

The little cat sounded happy too. I'm sure of it.

Jessica, her dad and the cat headed down the hall. I closed the door.

A crazy thing happened then. I felt happy and sad all at once. I guess Mom knew how I felt. She reached out and gave me a big hug.

"You did something very special, Robyn," said Mom.

That hug made me feel a whole lot better.

And do you know what? Next month, Jessica Johnson will bring Meow to school for My Life talks. I'm sure of it.

And I'll come up with something to talk about too. I don't own a lot of fancy things but I've got great ideas.

One of my best ideas was finding a home for the little cat.

That's me, Robyn.
That's My Life.

More new novels in the
New First Novels Series:

Jan's Awesome Party
Monica Hughes
Illustrated by Carlos Freire
Jan and Sarah are trying to figure out how to
spend the $40 they were given as a reward
for finding Patch. They settle on throwing a
party for their class -- a totally awesome
party. It's all set to go except they have to
have permission from the scary new
principal.

Carrie's Camping Adventure
Lesley Choyce
Illustrated by Mark Thurman
Carrie convinces her Mom to take her, her
brother and their two best friends on their
first-ever camping trip. When they get the
campsite in the provincial park their
misadventures begin when they find they
have forgotten to pack their food. The kids
are left alone for the rest of the day to put up
the tent and light a campfire and stay out of
mischief.

Great Play, Morgan

Ted Staunton

Illustrated by Bill Slavin

Morgan is persuaded by his friend Charlie to
sign up for soccer. He tells Aldeen Hummel
and she signs up too and the team blames
Morgan for making trouble. Aldeen brings
them too many penalties. Morgan wants to
quit. He's responsible for too many bad
things happening to the team.

Formac Publishing Company Limited
5502 Atlantic Street, Halifax, Nova Scotia B3H 1G4
Orders: 1-800-565-1975 Fax: (902) 425-0166